This
REA... ...ADY READ

My Reading Tree!

For Kate and Anna
~ E.B.
For Louise,
from Greg!

GLOUCESTERSHIRE COUNTY LIBRARY	
993241071 3	
PETERS	21-Nov-2008
	£4.99

LITTLE TIGER PRESS

An imprint of Magi Publications

1 The Coda Centre, 189 Munster Road,

London SW6 6AW

www.littletigerpress.com

This edition published 2008

First published in Great Britain 2005

Text copyright © Elizabeth Baguley 2005

Illustrations copyright © Magi Publications 2005

Elizabeth Baguley has asserted her right to be
identified as the author of this work under the
Copyright, Designs and Patents Act, 1988.

A CIP catalogue record for this book is available
from the British Library.

All rights reserved • Printed in China

ISBN 978-1-84506-666-6

2 4 6 8 10 9 7 5 3 1

MEGGIE
MOON

ELIzABETH BAGULEY

illustrated by
GREGOIRE MABIRE

LITTLE TIGER PRESS
London

Digger and Tiger spent all their time in the Yard. Nothing grew there but piles of dented things, empty things, worn-out things. No one else dared come to the Yard. It was *their* place.

Digger and Tiger were
rough-and-tumble boys,
spiky-haired, hole-at-the-knee
boys. They were not brothers,
but they went together like
a dustbin and its lid.

One day a girl arrived. She walked through the high gate and clicked it shut behind her. She stared at the tangled rubble and the king-of-the-castle boys. The boys stared back.

"I'm Meggie Moon," said the girl. "Can I play with you?"

"We don't play with girls," snarled Tiger.

"Girls don't know how to play," hissed Digger.

"Oh, don't they?" said Meggie, laughing.

Meggie left the boys standing in
the shadows and went to explore.
The Yard was a mess and the
boys were unfriendly, but Meggie
had ideas.

She picked up some of the
rubbish and began
to arrange it . . .

a tin here and

a pipe there . . .

until . . .

"It's a racing car!" said Tiger.
"You can drive it if you want,"
offered Meggie.
"Not likely," said Digger.

But as soon as Meggie left,
the boys jumped into the car
and raced away until dark.

The next day Meggie
came to the Yard again.
Digger and Tiger
watched her picking
over the junk.

"Go on, then, build
something!" ordered
Tiger.

So Meggie made
a ship. When it was
finished, the boys
played pirates.

"Can I come
aboard?" she asked.

"I suppose you
could be our cook,"
said Tiger.

"I'd rather be your lookout," said Meggie. She spat on her hands, shot up the rigging and shouted, "Enemy ship ahoy!" Startled, the boys drew their cutlasses. "Aye-aye, shipmate!" they said.

By the third day the
car was mangled and
the ship wrecked.

"Let's kick cans," said
Tiger.

"I'd rather throw
stones," whinged Digger.

"That's boring," said
Meggie. "Why don't we
make a den?"

She found wall-things
and roof-things and
the boys crammed and
jammed them into
a corner. They played
until dark, when the
bed calls came.

Every day
Meggie thought
of something different.
They crossed a snake pit,
shivered through a haunted
castle, lurched round
a roller-coaster . . .
    "She's not bad – for a
girl," Digger admitted
to Tiger, secretly.

Then, one day, Meggie announced,
"I'm going home tomorrow."
    The boys gazed at the Yard.
They remembered how, before Meggie
came, the rubble was just rubble.
    "But what shall we play?"
wailed Digger.

"I've brought you a goodbye present. You can play with that." Meggie wheeled in a towering load and toppled it in front of them.

"Star troops at the ready!" she commanded, then marched out through the gate, clicking it shut behind her.

"Aye-aye, Captain," Digger and Tiger saluted, but Meggie had gone. The sound of the closing gate echoed through the Yard.

The boys stared emptily after Meggie. At last they inched towards her present-pile. The heap of rubble was just . . . a porthole here, a jet there . . .

The boys looked at each other.

They had ideas.

"Star troops!" barked Digger.
"At the ready!" shouted Tiger.

By dusk, smooth things
and crumpled things,
shattered things and
battered things
spiralled high
above the
Yard fence.

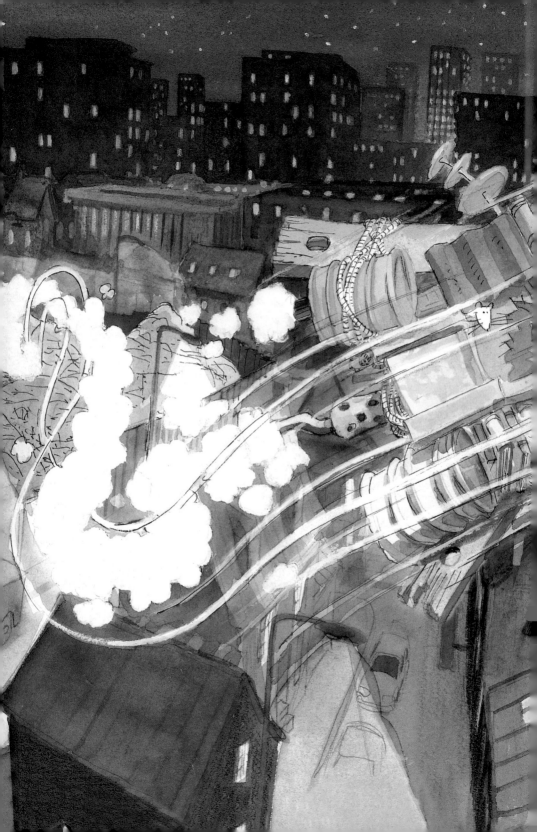

With spacesuits on, the astronauts climbed into the rocket.

"Blast off!" they chorused. With a roar and a rumble, the rocket burst into life and Digger and Tiger shot off skywards – away, away from the Yard in the Starship Meggie Moon.

Look at the words below and put the correct
picture stickers next to each word.

can

flag

flower

mouse

rubbish

sock

★ Have you got these right?
Then put a star on your reading tree!

Neat Nouns

A **noun** is a naming word – a person, place or thing. Add the missing nouns to the sentences below with the word stickers.

> rocket – gate – ship – astronauts – Yard – girl

1) Digger and Tiger spent all their time in the _____.

2) One day a _____ arrived.

3) So Meggie made a _____.

4) The sound of the closing _____ echoed through the Yard.

5) With spacesuits on, the _____ climbed into

the _____.

Can you find these sentences in the story?

★ Did you get all the nouns right? Great!
Add another star to your reading tree.

Super Search

Look at the picture below. Put the word stickers next to the correct objects in the picture. We've done one for you.

lid

★ When you have put all the words in the right places, add a star to your reading tree!

Drawing

Let's get creative! Draw a picture in the frame for each word below.

castle   dustbin   present

★ Did you draw all three pictures?
Add another star to your reading tree!

Lost Letters!

Oh no! Some of the letters in the words from the story have gone missing. Write the missing letter in each word, using the letters from the box.

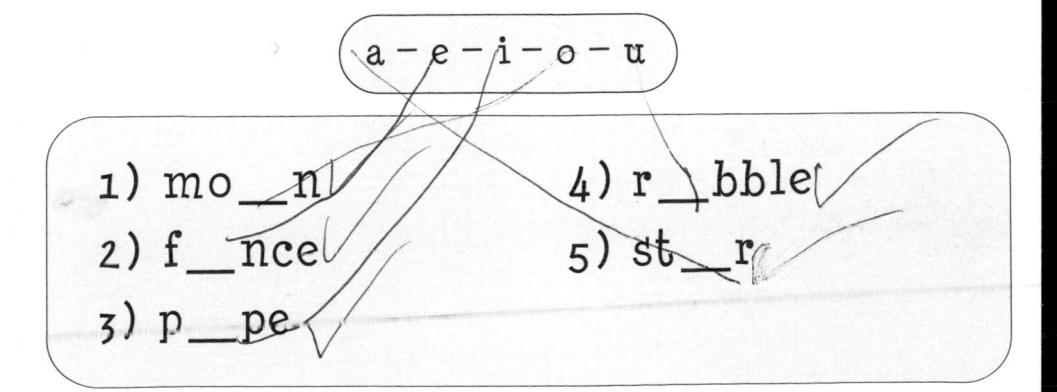

a – e – i – o – u

1) mo__n
2) f__nce
3) p__pe
4) r__bble
5) st__r

★ Could you spell the words right?
Don't forget to add another star to your reading tree!

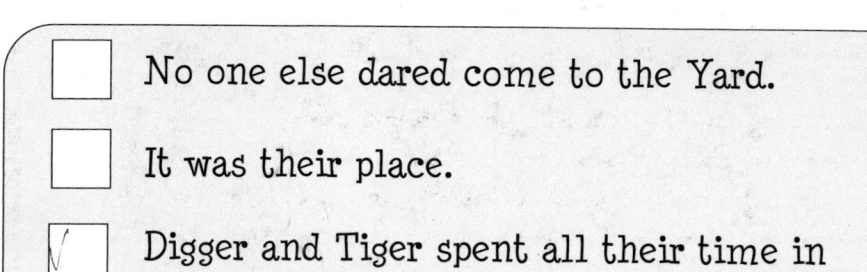

Sentence Order

All stories are made up of **sentences**. Tick the sentence below that came **first** in the story.

- [ ] No one else dared come to the Yard.
- [ ] It was their place.
- [✓] Digger and Tiger spent all their time in the Yard.

Cool Questions

Some sentences are questions. You know when a sentence is a question because it has a **question mark** at the end of it.

Put a **question mark** at the end of the sentences that are questions. Put a **full stop** at the end of the sentences that are not questions.

Can I play with you?

You can drive it if you want

Why don't we make a den?

But what shall we play?

You can play with that

⭐ Did you get the sentences and questions right?
Remember to add two more stars to your reading tree!